A catalogue record for this book is available from the British Library
Published by Ladybird Books Ltd
80 Strand London WC2R ORL
A Penguin Company

1 3 5 7 9 10 8 6 4 2

Animal Stories

Swinging Sally

written by Ronne Randall and Melanie Joyce

illustrated by John Haslam

Swinging Sally loved playing with her friends. She always looked forward to all the fun they had together.

Their favourite games
were round and round
the tree trunks...

catch the banana...

and swinging from the branches.

But Sally wasn't very good at swinging.
She just couldn't get the hang of it.
"Come and swing up here, Sally,"
her friends called out.
So she reached up, jumped...

and landed with a BUMP on
her bottom.
Sally felt really silly.
"It's no fun being a gorilla when you
can't swing from trees," she thought.

That afternoon, Sally asked her mum, "When will I be able to swing from the branches like other gorillas?"

"When your arms are strong enough," Mum told her. "You'll swing from the branches better than anyone, you wait and see!"

But Sally didn't want to wait and see.
She wanted to swing from the trees
right there and then.
So she reached up, jumped...and she
was nearly, just about,
almost, swinging when...

Oops!

down she came with a bumpety-
BUMP on her poor bottom.
"I don't like being a swingless
gorilla," she thought, grumpily.

At bedtime, Sally asked her dad,
"How can I get my arms to be strong
enough for swinging?"
"By getting lots of rest," said Dad.
"Come on now, it's time to go to sleep."

All night long, Sally dreamed of
swinging through the trees, using her
long, strong arms.

Early the next day, Sally rushed out
to find the biggest, tallest trees.
She reached up, jumped...and she
was nearly, just about, almost,
swinging when...

down she came with a bumpety-
bumpety-BUMP on her poor, sore,
lumpy bottom.
"I HATE being a gorilla," she growled,
and tore off into the trees.

Sally crashed her way through branches, bushes, leaves and trees. She was far too angry to notice Rhino fast asleep under a tree. "It's not fair!" she bellowed. "I just want to swing like the other gorillas." She reached up, jumped...and she was nearly, just about, almost, swinging when...

Rhino gave a snort and a grumpy grunt.
He turned to Sally with his beady eyes,
his pointy ears and his HUGE horn.
He was very angry. In fact, he
was FURIOUS!

Rhino stamped and charged. Sally ran and ran as fast as she could, but Rhino was closing in. He was nearly, almost, just about there when, suddenly, Sally reached up, jumped...and, yes, she was definitely, positively, easily, swinging and sweeping through the treetops!

She swept and swung all the way home. The other gorillas thumped their chests and cheered.

Sally was ready to play all the most fabulously swinging games.
"It's great being a gorilla," thought Sally.